MW01148971

Mail Order Bride

A Bride for Carlton

Sun River Brides
Book 1

Karla Gracey

Copyright © 2016 by Karla Gracey

All Rights Reserved. No part of this publication may be copied, reproduced in any format, by any means, electronic or otherwise, without prior consent from the copyright owner and publisher of this book.

This is a work of fiction. All characters, names, places and events are the product of the author's imagination or used fictitiously.

First Printing, 2016

Dedication

I dedicate this book to my mother, as she was the one who kept urging me to write, and without her enthusiasm I would never written and published my books.

Contents

Chapter One

Myra Gilbert sat in the nursery alone while her charges took their music lesson with Master Julian. She cherished these rare moments of solitude. So much of her life was taken up with caring for twelve year old Margaret and fourteen year old Carolynn. They were lovely girls, but boisterous and rarely sat still for a moment. But they would have no need of her soon enough and she wondered if she would ever find a position that was so amenable when the time came.

It had been the tragically early death of her dear Papa that had left her alone and with little to support herself with. Thankfully, as the daughter of the local Schoolmaster she had enjoyed the privilege of a good education, and so becoming a governess had seemed a most logical step. Now, after eight years with the Fitzherbert's she could feel her role had changed. She had no desire to remain with the family as simply a chaperone, though she had so loved teaching the girls. But there was little more she could impart to them now. They were young ladies; she had taught them to read and write, to draw, and they were good and kind. They would make excellent marriages, if only they could learn to curb their excessive exuberance for life.

She sighed heavily. She had once been just like her charges, dreaming of her future husband and children. She too had longed to be swept off her feet by a handsome young man who had eyes only for her – yet her chance had never come, and now she was destined for spinsterhood and a life as a governess. She wished she didn't mind, but she had yet to reconcile herself to her fate. She still hoped, against all the odds, that there was love and a family in her future. But as each year passed, that hope became less and less strong. It was now but a mere flicker in her heart. But she enjoyed her work, and that was a consolation to her, and her girls had won her heart and her devotion.

A newspaper sat on the table to her side, and she picked it up - surprised to find that it wasn't the usual Daily Bugle – but the Matrimonial Times. She could only presume that there must have been some mistake with the delivery that morning, the Fitzherbert's would have no need of such a publication after all. Intrigued, she flicked through the pages, amused by the pleas of lonely farmers, ranchers, miners and their like. So many of them sounded so very like her after all; lonely and feeling that time had passed them by. She could feel the pain in so many of the words, and her heart went out to them. But though she so desperately longed for a family of her own she could not understand how any woman could ever bring herself to respond to such advertisements; heading off to who knew where to live with men they knew little to nothing about. No, she prayed she would find a man using more traditional means, though she was beginning to think it unlikely. She was fast heading towards the spinsterhood she so dreaded; at twenty-seven she was often passed over at social events for the younger and wealthier young women of her acquaintance.

She was about to put the newspaper down and go in search of her novel, when she caught sight of an advertisement that seemed completely unusual, though she only had this morning's perusal of the publication to judge. She read it once, then again, and again:

A Gentleman of Montana, wishes to enter into a correspondence with a view to matrimony; she must be gentle, kind and full of courage. A liberal education, and love of theatre and music would be highly prized, and to be a fine cook and care for hearth and home would be preferred. The subscriber is a man of modest means, with land of his own and believes that he has qualities that such a woman would appreciate. Address in Sincerity E.T.C., Box 483, Matrimonial Times

So many of the advertisements that she had skimmed over had been almost gushing in their sentimentality, yet this one was not. It gave no clue as to the character or habits of the man who had submitted it in the hope of attracting a wife. It seemed almost cold, unfeeling. She was sure that it would have been unlikely to catch the eye of many women, who seemed to want romance more than the things that would truly last. Not that she thought marriage should be a mercenary act, but a good home and friendship would stand a couple in far better stead than hearts and flowers she was sure. Yet, for some reason the words resonated within her, and she felt a brief flutter of excitement deep in her belly.

Hardly believing that she was doing so, with her curiosity getting the better of her, she began to pen a letter to the mysterious man who had put himself unwittingly into her line of sight. She scribbled hastily, barely heeding a word she wrote, and then sealed her missive in an envelope and addressed it carefully. She tucked it into her reticule and rushed out of the house to the postal office. She barely dared to catch a breath, barely took a moment to think until she walked back outside and realized what she had done. What if he replied? Even worse, what if he did not?

* * * * *

Carlton Green stared at the stark black and white print of his advertisement. It shocked him to see how foolish it seemed to be doing such a thing, now he saw it nestled within the pages of this ridiculous newspaper. Whatever had he been thinking, to advertise for a wife in such a way? He could see nothing in it that could interest a young woman worth having; in fact he thought it made him sound pompous and unlikeable indeed. He seemed to expect much of a wife and yet was offering her nothing in return. He had slaved over the words for days, had thought he

3

had chosen so carefully, and yet now they looked dull and expectant. Exasperated, he threw the newspaper into the fire certain he would have no replies, and got on with his chores. There was time enough for him to find a wife – but the sowing would not get done on its own.

He held enough land to eke out a comfortable living, but it was hard. He worked from sun up to sun down, no matter the weather. He grew oats and some wheat on his one hundred and sixty acres, granted to him now in perpetuity thanks to the Homestead Act. He often wondered how he had stayed the course required to be granted the deeds to his lands. But despite some very difficult times, terrible harvests and having to work himself to the bone he had done so. Many had failed, their steadings had been left abandoned as disease and the sheer enormity of the task had become clear to those with less hardy natures than his own. He had lost many friends to the cemetery, and even more back to the lives they had left behind thinking that the opportunities here in Montana would be better. He missed them, and life out here miles from the nearest town could be all too quiet. It was time to settle down and make this land a home, and so his search for a wife had begun. He needed somebody to share in his good fortune, to care for and to protect, and to fill his life with joy and laughter.

He was still here, and he was not just surviving – he had begun to truly thrive - and it was now time to settle down and make Montana a home as well as an adventurous enterprise. Stepping outside into the warm sunshine, he gazed proudly at his neatly furrowed fields, and the large yard that would make a wonderful playground for young children. The paddock held horses and ponies that needed to be ridden, and the peace and quiet ached to be rent with the sound of fun and family. Then he turned and looked behind him at the ramshackle cabin he had laid his head down in for the past five years, and laughed. His dreams may seem achievable when he looked at everything else he had – but he could hardly expect any woman to wish to live there. The sod cabin was just a room; it had no windows and the chimney belched smoke so badly he had to put out the fire over night to ensure he didn't choke in his sleep.

He vowed to head into Sun River to speak with Ardloe Reed once the spring sowing was done. The carpenter had built many of his neighbors some sturdy looking homes in recent months, and it was time he did the same. He could have no illusions that any young woman seeing how he currently lived – without having been entirely enamored of him - would be right on the next train out of Great Falls or Billings before he could stop her. He chuckled wryly as he thought of some Eastern city girl hitching up her skirts and making a run for it, it seemed most unlikely but it amused him nonetheless.

He shrugged his oilskin jacket on as he crossed the yard. The air in the barn was cold no matter the time of year, and he was glad of the hardwearing coat and his second best hat to keep the worst of the chill breezes from tearing through to his skin. He blew on his fingers to warm them before lifting a sack of seed. He'd check it over and then get going. He had three more fields to sow with wheat today, and a further four with oats tomorrow. Half his fields needed to see the run of the plough still too. He whistled as he began to stack the sacks of seed onto the cart, enjoying the brief respite from the cold that he got from being in the spring sunshine. He hitched Marlin, his broad-backed and sturdy cart horse into the shafts and with a click, and a swift flick of the whip to the reliable animal's flanks, the two of them set off to the high fields.

Carlton loved the land he had chosen with all his heart. He had been lucky enough to take his pick. There had been so few homesteaders coming out this far when he first arrived, but he didn't doubt that more would come, especially if the rumors turned out to be true that the Government wanted to extend the scope of the Homesteading Act. The land was fertile, both crops and livestock seemed to thrive here if you worked hard enough. Men who were hungry for success and weren't afraid to work for it could do very well here.

But his was a lonely life. Many of his contemporaries, those brave few that had come out here to try and make new lives, had brought wives and children with them or at the least sent for them once they had gotten settled. The transition could be harsh, and many families had not managed to secure the deeds to their lands. He was proud he now had his securely stored in the vaults of the Great Falls bank - and that he had done so alone. But he longed for companionship now the lands were in good heart and he could afford to hire some help. At least that was a task that would be easy to fulfill. There were always men looking for work at the Saloon in Sun River, and even as far away as Great Falls and Billings. Eager young souls arrived on the train every day.

Carlton longed for sons, to bring up and to show what life could be like if you worked hard and earned your rewards; to work alongside him on the farm to create a family empire and so in his loneliness had placed that advertisement. He couldn't help but regret having done so now as he thought about how cold he had sounded against the other Matrimonials he had spied on the page near his own. Maybe that was to be expected. Maybe Fate had taken a stand as he had penned his own words, to ensure he would remain alone.

After all, he wasn't entirely sure that he should ever be a husband or father given his checkered history. He had made such a mess of it all the first time around, had caused such pain that it hardly bore thinking of. But that was the past, and he prayed every day that his loneliness here in Montana could make up for his past digressions, that his commitment to the earth would somehow redeem him. That he would one day deserve the happiness so long denied him.

Chapter Two

Once the ploughing and sowing was finally complete Carlton managed to make a trip into town. It felt good to have a little bit of energy left at the end of the day to go and relax with friends. "Just the fella I needed to see," Carlton called across the street as he spied Ardloe staggering out of the Saloon. The old man wasn't much of a drinker, but when the weather was cold his arthritis played him up and made him limp a little. One or two whiskeys and it became almost dangerous for the old coot to be out anywhere alone. Carlton had helped him up off the ground on more than one occasion as carriages and buggies came at him too fast and knocked him off his shaky limbs.

"Whatever it is can't it wait 'til the mornin'?" the crusty carpenter grumbled.

"I won't be in town in the morning my friend, but I am here now. I'm in need of a new house."

"Sure y'are. Ev'yone in town's in need, so they keep on tellin' me anyhow."

"Can you do it Ardloe, or should I ask that young fella from down the valley?" Carlton knew full well that threatening to bring in the competition would rile him up, and he was right.

"Sure I can do it, no need to bring in that slipshod fool. Thinks he can build a house, can't even build a henhouse!" Carlton chuckled and Ardloe looked at him with the dawning comprehension that he had just been hustled. "Green, you have a mighty nasty sense of humor. But, I'll build ya a nice house. When d'ya want it done by?"

"Soon as you can. You just let me know what you need and I will make sure it is all ready for and waiting for you."

"I'll send ya a list," the old man said grudgingly. "Now, may I go home to my wife and some liniment for these aches and pains?" Carlton patted him on the back, and watched as he limped slowly across the street towards a smart little clapboard home. It was typical of all Ardloe's work; neat, precise and downright sturdy. They truly were built to last. "Oh, Postmaster was looking for you earlier. Something about a letter from Boston?" the old man said over his shoulder as he went inside.

Carlton swiveled on his heel, as the door slammed shut - stunned. The newspaper's offices were in Boston, but surely it would just be a letter telling him that they were sorry but his advertisement had yielded no responses and they needed his box for another subscriber? Yet his heart gave a little leap, hope refusing to die. It would be so much easier if it would. He tipped his hat at his friend and headed inside to see what he might find.

When things weren't too busy at the farm Carlton came into town no more than once a week to have a few drinks, and maybe play some cards with his neighbors, but mostly he was just too tired to do much more. During early spring and round the harvest he rarely even made it to church. He knew that if there was mail for farmers like himself it was often left behind the bar at the Saloon so he tried not to leave it too long to drop by. The arrangement made for an easier system; no long and drawn out deliveries for the Postmaster, and no need to get into town during office hours for men who worked all the hours God was good enough to send them. Just knowing that Tom would hold his correspondence until he dropped by was a huge help.

"Green, I got some mail for you," Tom said as he served him a mug of ale. Carlton slipped his money over the counter and waited as the lanky Saloon owner brought him the letter. The envelope felt heavy and substantial in his hand. His bright and ambitious friend grinned at him, a knowing look in his eyes. Tom had come out here when there were only the trappers and miners brave enough to take the trip. He'd brought good looking girls and good beer and whiskey at cheap prices. His success had been assured from the off. But, he could be too observant sometimes – though he was also highly discrete.

"Thanks, is the back room taken?" Carlton asked, wanting a little privacy to open the letter. He didn't want his friends to think him soft, if he showed his disappointment – and he certainly didn't wish for the teasing that might follow if any of them found out what he had done. He knew that Tom wouldn't tell a soul, but the same could not be said of some of the other faces in the bar.

"Empty for about half an hour, but the Women's Suffrage meeting will be starting then, so best to get yourself out of their way," Tom said rolling his eyes. Carlton winked at him companionably, but unlike so many men Carlton strongly agreed that women should have the vote. They worked as hard out here as any man, harder than many – and bringing up children was no easy task either. They deserved a say in how the Government was run, it affected their lives as much as any man's after all. Secretly he considered them to be far wiser than his own sex too – he had never yet known a woman who had gotten herself into the sorts of scrapes he did on a regular basis.

He walked through into the large reception room, and ripped open the envelope. Inside was a letter on flimsy paper, with the address of the newspaper stamped across it. He flicked his eye over it, and saw much as he had expected to see, that his box was now required by another and that unfortunately they could no longer keep it open for him. It had been three months and he was a realist – if he was going to receive a response he supposed he would have done so by now. But a second envelope was also included. He looked back at the last line of the letter he had only barely read, and saw that they had included the single response he had received, and that they wished him much luck with it.

He felt his chest constrict with fear as he wondered what kind of woman could possibly have responded to him. She would either have to be desperate, or downright unpleasant, he was sure of that. But as he took a deep breath and opened up the thick parchment envelope and took out the soft and creamy paper inside, he tried to gulp down his anxieties. Maybe she would be perfect, maybe it was a sign that there truly was only one woman for every man after all?

Dear Gentleman of Montana,

Please forgive my being so bold as to reply to your advertisement. I was not brought up to do such a thing, but I find myself alone and without guidance as to what may be proper in such a situation as this.

I am sure you have probably received many responses; your advertisement struck me as the only one I read which could truly have been said to be honest. Though, I want you to know I do not regularly peruse such a tome. I am still not even sure how it was in the house, but I was intrigued and simply could not help myself from writing to you. I don't know what came over me.

I am governess to two young women who are nearly old enough to come out and find husbands and lives of their own. My Papa died when I was just seventeen, my Mama just after I was born. Papa was a Schoolmaster, and he insisted I have as good an education as the boys he taught. He believed a day would come when women would finally achieve the place in Society that they deserved –not as simply ornaments. But, you do not wish to hear of my Papa's politics, I am sure.

I have always longed for a family of my own, though I am past the age of expecting to be able to command exclamations of undying love. Nor do I crave romance. But I would love to have my own home, and a husband who might permit me to teach in a local school so I can continue to use my education to prosper other young women – and if there is no provision for them in Montana, to maybe set up a school for girls myself.

I have no dowry but myself. I am hardworking and used to hardship. I am told by my charges and their wonderful parents, my employers, that I am kind and good as your advertisement requested, but I couldn't possibly be so immodest as to say so myself.

I have read about Montana in the newspapers, of course, and I understand it is a place of great beauty. I should very much love to see it with my own eyes. At present I travel only through my storybooks and the wonderful travelers' tales that get printed in the newspapers here in Boston. I do love music and theatre, and I forever have my nose in a book. I can cook, though it has been some time since I needed to – but I did keep house for my Papa from a very young age. I like to think that household management skills are amongst those that you never forget.

I fear this has been a terribly garbled account of myself, and probably barely even scratches the surface. Should you wish to know any more I would be much inclined to answer any questions you may have. Please, do write to me and tell me of your life in Montana, and maybe even a little about why you would like a wife – your advertisement was very hazy on the details after all!

Yours in Sincerest Hope

Myra Gilbert

Carlton stared at the elegant script that had clearly been written hurriedly as the page was covered in ink splatters and crossings out. He couldn't take the smile from his face, this woman most certainly had a sense of humor, and she was eager and keen. He could sense the urgency of her response; it was as if she had simply written the entire letter without taking a breath. Quickly he downed his ale and rushed through the Saloon and into the street where he had left Canton, his horse. Unhitching him quickly he raced back to the farm to pen his response.

* * * * *

Myra stared at the envelope sat on the silver salver by her plate at breakfast. She rarely received much correspondence, but it was not that which had so perturbed her. It was the sender's address, so neatly penned in a simple and unadorned script that had taken her breath away. It had come from Montana. It had come from him. And his name was Carlton Green. She rolled the name around in her mind, foolishly even trying it out for size, Myra Green sounded quite respectable and fine.

As the girls clattered in to the room and took their seats she shook her head to rid herself of such foolish notions, and scolded them tenderly. "Alice, Grace must you always behave like hoydens? I am sure that both your Mama and myself have taught you better."

"Apologies Miss Gilbert," they chorused, grinning madly. Myra chuckled.

"I can always get my revenge, that is where the two of you can be so foolish," she reminded them. "I think Latin immediately after breakfast, and maybe mathematics to follow."

"You wouldn't, not on such a glorious day," Alice said aghast. "Surely today should be about biology; capturing frogspawn and learning about nature?" Both girls were bright as a button. If they were boys they would both be preparing to enter the university. Myra thought it terribly unfair that such enquiring minds would be lost within marriage, and so soon.

"You are right, I would not," she reassured them both. "But, we shall not be going to the park, but to the zoological gardens. I hear they have some wonderful new animals for us to learn about." She was rewarded with squeals of delight. "Now, eat up and then you shall need to get your coats and hats so we can enjoy as much of the day there as possible."

She watched them carefully as they ate; giving gentle nudges to remind them of etiquette they were forgetting and ensuring that they remembered to leave just a little on their plates. She insisted that they rise gracefully from their places and walk elegantly up to their rooms. She knew that they would race up the stairs however much she tried to exhort otherwise, but every little bit of ladylike comportment she could insist upon she would.

As the peace descended around her once more she looked back at her letter. She simply couldn't wait until they returned from their excursion to know what Mr. Carlton Green wished to say to her. She clutched it to her heart and prayed his words would be kindly. Carefully she slit the envelope with the ivory handled knife laid out on the salver for her. She carefully extracted the paper, and laid the envelope back down neatly. Taking a deep breath, she began to read the scruffy script. It was a little difficult to make out at times, but it pleased her nonetheless.

Dear Miss Gilbert,

I cannot tell you how delighted I was to receive your letter. I shudder to make you blush, but it seemed that you must have written it in a hurry? I wonder if writing to me was something that made you perhaps a little nervous, as writing to you now is for me. I must confess I have screwed up many sheets of paper and fed my fire well to get even this far.

I enjoyed hearing of your work; you seem very enamored of it. I think it is good to be passionate about what one does. It must run in your blood, what with your Papa being a School Master. I am passionate about my land. I work hard because it inspires me to do so. I am a farmer, and I grow mainly oats and wheat, though I do have some vegetable crops too. The soil is good here, fertile and rich.

I do not mind your talk of politics, though I understand it is often considered rude in polite society. I too think it important, that anyone who has the ability to do so should be able to learn. I must confess to you that I am a secret supporter of the suffrage movement too – though I ask you to kindly keep it to yourself, my compatriots out here aren't all so amenable to the thought! Isn't it strange how writing makes it so much easier to impart confidences?

You wished to hear more about me, and Montana. There is little to know about me – I have little time to be anything other than a busy farmer. But as it may have been clear from my advertisement, I do love music and I especially love intellectual discourse. I should be glad to continue a correspondence with someone as clearly well informed as yourself, and hope that by doing so I will learn much.

Montana however is a different story. It is vast, and the terrain can be rugged in parts. The mountains are more than majestic – they make you feel small, so humble and yet closer to God somehow. My farm is situated in the most glorious of valleys and the views all around are breathtaking. The blues never seemed so blue back East, the greens dull and tired in comparison. Everything seems brighter, fresher and clearer out here.

I am building a house, or rather my friend Ardloe is building me a house. For too long I have lived in a shack not truly fit for habitation of neither man nor beast. He showed me a drawing of what he thinks it will look like once he is done. It will be very fine. There shall be four large bedrooms, a smart parlor, a vast kitchen and even an indoor outhouse! Should we decide that we might suit I should be most grateful of your assistance in furnishing it and making of it a real home – I hope you do not think me too presumptuous in such a request?

As to your possible occupation should you wish to join me here, there is a school in Great Falls, and one in Billings too – for boys only as far as I am aware. Sun River is much smaller, but people are content to travel for an education. I am sure that the townsfolk would be more than happy for you to set up a local school – though I must warn you that there are many here who would disapprove of educating women. However the local Women's Suffrage group I am sure would assist you, and I would be more than happy to give you my support in doing so.

I feel I may be rushing things terribly, but do you think you might consider me? I am not perfect and I can assure you that living here will not be easy, but I have the most wonderful feeling that we just might suit.

I look forward eagerly to your response, and pray you will not be scared off by my ardor.

Yours Most Sincerely

Carlton Green

P.S. May I please call you Myra? It is such a lovely name!

Myra hugged the letter to her breast, after pressing it gently to her lips. He had not been put off by her ridiculously hasty response. In fact, it seemed to her that her impetuousness was exactly the thing that appealed to him about her, and it would appear that he had a similar streak inside him too. She longed to be able to send a reply immediately, but the girls were now stood in the doorway looking smart and presentable in their coats, hats and gloves and so she tucked the letter safely into her reticule and stood up to join them. "Are you both ready?" she asked smiling at them both, her heart light with joy and hope. They nodded eagerly. "Then let us go and see the animals."

Chapter Three

Despite how much work he had to undertake, Carlton seemed to find more and more reasons as to why he must go in to town after he received Myra's first letter. He tried to tell himself that it truly was because he needed to speak with Ardloe about plans for the house, or to arrange the deliveries of seed he needed, and the materials for the house of course. But, he knew in his heart that it was because he kept praying there would be another letter from her waiting for him at the Saloon. It seemed to be taking an age to hear from her.

But on a crisp spring morning, just as he had finally sown the seeds in the last of his fields, her next missive appeared. Her beautiful sloping script brought a surge of pleasure to his heart, and relief as he had begun to wonder if he had somehow managed to put her off.

Dear Mr Green, Carlton

Why of course you must call me Myra, and I shall gladly call you Carlton if I may. It would be too peculiar to be talking of marriage with someone who could only ever bring themselves to be so formal and polite. I am so glad that you think we may suit. I am not perfect either and would never expect a husband to be so. We are all human and have our little foibles after all.

Your description of Montana makes me long to visit there. I have never been outside of the city before, but I am sure that I would suit a country life. I have never felt at home here, it is too busy and crowded, though it is wonderful to have the concert halls, theatres and museums to visit. I think I long for open spaces. I take the girls to the park every single day – whatever the weather. They often grumble terribly if it is cold or wet!

Oh, and I would be so happy to teach a small local school. The children could gain so much more from it than having to travel long distances to learn – and of course I would hope that their parents could see the benefits of them being so close too, that they would have more time to study or to help out at home if they did not have to go so far to school. I am so glad that you would support me in such an endeavor. I truly could not give it up I don't think.

You must be doing very well indeed to be planning such a house – with an indoor outhouse of all things! You will be telling me next that you intend to have electricity installed throughout too! I am sure your current home is not the hovel you cite, but if it truly is then I am glad that there will be something a little more comfortable. I am not sure that I could manage to live in a sod built shack. I have been living in a very fine town house here in Boston, though of course only in the servant's quarters, but it would be quite a change otherwise.

I am not afraid of hardship though, merely a little apprehensive about the unknown. Maybe you could come and visit me, so we could see if we would suit? It would put my mind at rest to know that should we wed that I could at least rely upon my husband to care for me and help my adjustment. I can arrange for you to stay at Young's Hotel, it is quite fine and has a good reputation and is only a couple of blocks from my home. We could maybe attend the theatre and undertake some excursions?

Though of course, I am being ever so presumptuous, as you are probably very busy at this time of year and would have no time to just take off for a period of weeks just to put my mind at ease. I would understand if it were not possible. I suppose I could even come to Montana, but that would mean I would have to leave my position and it would be hard to find such a good one should we decide we do not like one another in the flesh.

I am sorry, dear Carlton, I am blathering on about nothing of consequence and must be boring you. I shall stop now before I embarrass myself further. I do look forward to your next letter, and I pray we will meet in person very soon.

Yours hopefully

Myra

Carlton's heart had taken a little leap as he read her witty response to his request to use her Christian name, but had lurched into his boots as she spoke of foibles. He wondered if she would ever be able to accept his. He had done so well to keep them from his mind, to build a life once more without his failings being known. But, if they were to marry, surely it would be better to be honest, to be truthful with her of his past?

But he wasn't sure he could be. What if she turned away from him, and no longer wished to even correspond with him? It had been such a short acquaintance, but he already treasured her words more than anything. He simply could not, would not, imagine a life without her. But that meant he would have to ensure that everything about his history remained hidden from view forever. Was that even possible? He knew all too well that bad news always travelled – and just because it hadn't caught up with him yet did not mean that it wouldn't some day.

He longed to do just as she asked, to join her in Boston, to see the sights. He was in the perfect position to. All of his sowing was done. He could afford to hire someone to oversee the farm while he was gone, while there was little that had to be completed. It would be the ideal time to do so. Yet, there was a gnawing in his belly that told him that no good could ever come of this. He had left the East for a new start, in a place where nobody knew him. Returning to the world that had so broken him would be the hardest thing he had ever done – yet he could not expect her to come to him. It would not be right for a woman to cross the country alone, heaven alone knew the dangers that she would have to face.

No, if he wanted Myra to become his wife then he would have to go to her. He would have to hope that he had reformed himself sufficiently that nobody would ever recognize him as the man who had left all those years before – that nobody would tell her his secrets, at least not before he had been able to gauge if she would ever forgive him should she know it all.

* * * * *

Myra had become a fidget. She only prayed that her employers had not noticed it. She was on edge constantly, waiting for another letter to come from Carlton. She hoped he would not think her too forward for virtually demanding that he come here to meet with her. She couldn't remember ever having been so forceful about anything in her life. Yet, there had been so little in her life that she had wanted so badly. She knew it was foolish, and she knew that she knew so very little about him – yet still she knew she loved him. She simply couldn't bear the idea of living her life without him now, and though that was terribly exciting it was also frightening too.

Myra's life had been a lonely one, and to combat the losses she had turned to her books. Suddenly they were no solace to her as every night she was assailed with dreams of becoming Carlton's wife. Of making his lovely new house into a comfortable and loving home for him and their children. She was barely managing to maintain discipline over the girls, as she became less and less connected to her life here. Her lack of care would soon be noticed, and then she would be out on the streets without a character, and if Carlton did not make her his bride that would be disastrous.

She bit at her nails, as she re-read his last letter. His words were warm and friendly. He had seemed even jovial. She pored over every syllable, trying to find a reason not to trust him, not to give her heart to him and she found none. He seemed good and kind, generous and clever –

everything she had ever longed for in a husband. She had never known just how much she longed to be free of her current life until now. Just a few short months ago she had believed herself to be content and now she longed for the mountains and clear skies he spoke of with such affection.

Her reverie was broken by a knock on her door. "Miss Gilbert?" Annie, the chamber maid, called. "There is a young gentleman caller for you Miss," she said as Myra opened the door.

"A gentleman caller? But I am expecting no-one," she said puzzled. The only person who ever called for her was Mrs Cartwright, the Minister's wife. They took tea together on Myra's day off.

"He is ever so handsome Miss," Annie said with a grin. "I'd be ever so happy if he came a callin' for me!"

"Get back to work Annie, less of that nonsense," Myra scolded gently. She quickly smoothed her hair back and secured it with a couple of extra pins in the practical bun she always wore. There was only one person she could think of who might come calling on her without having announced a visit beforehand; only one person in her life who seemed so impetuous. But it couldn't be him? Carlton would have had to have left the very morning he received her last letter to have gotten here this quickly.

Her heart full of hope though, she ran down the stairs, curious as to who had come to ask for her, nervous that it may be just who she believed it to be. Whoever it was had clearly upset Mr Graham, the butler, as he had come to the front door. She stifled a giggle as she saw his stern face.

"Miss Gilbert, please ensure that your friends know to call for you at the servants entrance in future please."

"Of course, I do hope you haven't left him on the doorstep though?" she asked looking around and seeing no sign of a caller.

"Of course not. I had him sent to the rear parlor. He did not give me a card so I cannot tell you who he might be."

"Thank you Mr Graham, I shall see what he wants and send him on his way."

"That would be best," he said haughtily as he turned sharply and stalked off down the corridor towards the library. Myra could hold it in no longer, and she laughed out loud. He truly could be such a pompous prig.

She hurried to the little parlor that the staff used to read or unwind in quiet moments of the day. There were few of them, and so it was rarely used. She hesitated before she opened the door to enter. She truly did wonder who would be on the other side of it though she knew the only way to find out would be to enter. She took a deep breath, trying to calm the jumble of butterflies that seemed to have overtaken her entire torso, and turned the handle.

A tall, broad shouldered man stood at the mantle. He wore a black Stetson and boots, and a smartly tailored suit. The combination was strangely incongruous – and yet it suited him well. His obviously muscular body filled out the grey cotton and silk blend beautifully; his slim hips and flat stomach letting the fabric glide in the most flattering way. Whoever he was, he was quite the physical specimen. Her heart began to flutter, sure that her dreams had come true – that Carlton was here, in Boston, for her!

She coughed politely to alert him to her presence, he turned. She was struck dumb by the greenest eyes she had ever seen. Mesmerized she could hardly catch her breath. "Miss Gilbert? Myra Gilbert?" he asked her tentatively. She nodded, her throat suddenly so dry she feared she wouldn't get even the most simple of words out. "I am so sorry for the intrusion, but once you said you wished for me to visit, I simply couldn't bear to waste any time. I was on the first train out of Great Falls, and so here I am."

"Indeed, "she managed to croak as he took her hands in his and searched her face eagerly. She moistened her lips and swallowed a few times. "How was your journey?" she asked foolishly. He grinned at her.

"It was very enjoyable, just knowing I was on my way to meet you made it fly by. But I can see my presence has disconcerted you. Would you like me to leave? I can go to the hotel and give you time to process things should you wish?" Myra was touched by his consideration. But now he was here she didn't want to let him out of her sight. He was such a picture to gaze upon after all, with his chiseled jaw and smiling eyes.

"No, let me get us some tea and we can sit down and talk," she said hurriedly, as she backed out of the tiny room slowly.

She shut the door on him reluctantly, and walked a few steps towards the kitchen. Suddenly she found herself gasping for breath. She stopped, and leant against the wall, pressing her forehead to the cool plaster. He was simply too perfect. Whatever would he see in a woman like her? She was too plain, too dull, and too ordinary for any man who looked that good to ever consider. "Stop that," she commanded herself as she tried to pull herself together. "You are as good as any woman, and better than many. Any man would be lucky to call you his wife." She didn't believe her words, but she tried to imagine them the way her Papa had always said them, and knew he had believed every word.

"Cook, could you possibly prepare me afternoon tea for two please?"

"Annie said you have a visitor. Do you need me to come and act as chaperone?" the portly woman asked with a teasing smile.

"I think I am old enough to take care of my virtue Cook, but I am grateful for the offer," Myra responded cheekily.

"Is he truly as handsome as she said?"

"That would depend upon your definition of handsome I suppose," Myra said thoughtfully. "If you think a city boy with a fancy moustache and slicked back hair to be handsome then you would be sadly disappointed, but if your tastes run to a rangy cowboy, all muscle, with wicked green eyes, rumpled hair and a lopsided smile then he might be for you!"

"Sounds like you are smitten already. However did you meet him?" Cook bustled around as she asked questions, putting together a tray worthy of royalty. She laid out cakes and scones, sandwiches and a large silver teapot.

"I didn't. I have never seen him before today," Myra said honestly, trying to dodge the personal question. Cook had already spotted that she liked him and found him attractive. She would have to be very careful not to give anything away until she knew where she stood with the devilishly handsome man awaiting her in the parlor. "Now, if I may I shall go and find out what he has come to see me about," she said as she picked up the tray and made her way back to the man she prayed above all else would become her husband, and soon.

Chapter Four

Carlton was grateful for the moment of respite. Seeing Myra in the flesh had surpassed all of his wildest imaginings. She had a trim figure, and the biggest blue eyes that he had ever seen. The neat blonde hair looked as though it would be long and curling, if the wisps around her cheeks were anything to go by, but he couldn't be entirely sure until he had the pleasure of unpinning it and letting it fall down her slender back in waves. Yet, she seemed to have no idea of her physical impact upon men. He had known beautiful women before, they tended to walk into a room with the confidence that they can have whatever they desire-Myra did not have that arrogance. She seemed almost timid in fact.

He took the opportunity to gather his thoughts, and to try and calm the purely physical reaction that had occurred as he had taken her hands. It had felt as if a bolt of lightning had shot through him, setting every part of him on high alert. He wanted her; that was without doubt. He thought he had seen a flicker of desire in her eyes too – he prayed he wasn't just deceiving himself, seeing what he longed to see. He hadn't expected to find love, much less passion when he had advertised for a wife. At best he had hoped for companionship. So, to find a woman he was clearly so attracted to physically was more than he could ever have imagined.

His breath caught once more as she re-entered the room. "Here, let me help you with that," he offered taking the tray from her hands. She smiled at him nervously. "I won't bite Myra, I promise."

"That is good to know," she said bravely. "It would be ever so difficult to explain after all." He grinned. That was good, the feisty woman from the letters was in there, he had just taken her by surprise. "Now, how do you take your tea?"

"Hot and black," he said and chuckled as she looked at him in surprise.

"No milk, no sugar?"

"I ran out one day, drank it anyhow and never really worried about it since," he admitted. "I don't often have a lot of time, and it just makes things a bit easier. I am sorry I turned up out of the blue, I should have written to say I was coming."

"Please don't apologize, it was a wonderful shock. I should have guessed – our correspondence has been impulsive on both sides from the start." She smiled and handed him an elegant china cup. Her entire face lit up as she did so, revealing cute dimples that he just longed to kiss.

"So, will it be convenient for me to stay for a few days so we might see if we suit?" he asked boldly.

"It would. Something is clearly working in our favor, as the girls are currently away with their parents in Europe and so my duties are much reduced. I have all the time in the world to show you Boston," she said eagerly.

"That is fortuitous indeed," he agreed. "But, I came from a little place not far from here. I know Boston quite well, and so I already have us tickets for the opera this evening. I do hope you like Mozart?"

"I do indeed, I so wanted to attend the performances of Don Giovanni – but the tickets were prohibitively expensive," she said, her little rosebud mouth open in shock. Unable to resist, he reached out and gently pushed her chin up to close it. He stroked her cheek. It was soft, and yielding. She shuddered gently at his touch, then pulled away hastily. "I could not possibly let you spend such an amount on me."

"I didn't. I spent it on myself – I would just like you to accompany me." He took her chin in his hand once more and held her head so he could stare deeply into her eyes. "You won't leave me to the mercy of all the Boston socialites alone?" he begged. She shook her head out of his grasp and laughed nervously.

"Of course I wouldn't. But are you truly sure?"

"Myra, I have just travelled across the country to see you. I intend to spend as much time with you as I possibly can for that was the very purpose of my visit. If I can add in some theatre, a few museums and the opera whilst doing so I shall consider this trip perfection."

* * * * *

Myra had never blushed quite so furiously in her life. She had been glad to hurry him off to the hotel so she could bathe and dress for the evening's entertainment, simply because she had been sure that she would soon go up in flames - her face had felt so hot. His compliments had seemed genuine enough, yet she couldn't quite bring herself to believe him. She saw her image in the mirror every day, she was no socialite beauty. She was a simple woman, with simple tastes. But, Carlton was not simple. He was intelligent, funny and too good looking for her to trust herself.

She had already fallen for him in his letters; to meet him in the flesh had been overwhelming. She did not know if she would be able to survive the rejection that would be sure to come as he got to know her and decided that he wanted someone younger, prettier, less determined to be independent. She would be unable to temper that in herself. Her work was important to her, and she truly believed that women deserved more than they settled for in life. Few men were able to accept that, let alone encourage it in their wives.

She looked at the gowns in her closet. She owned three: her cornflower blue, for Sunday best; her grey cotton for in the school room; and her cream velvet for outings during the day. None of them was suitable for a night at the Opera. She sighed and sank onto her bed. There was no time to have one made, no time to even purchase something from one of the department stores as they would all now be closed for the day. She held up her blue gown against her, and looked at herself in the mirror. It would have to do.

"Miss Gilbert, Miss Gilbert, there's a package for you," Annie yelled excitedly as she burst into the room without knocking. Myra tried to look at her sternly, but Annie's eyes were alight with pleasure and she simply couldn't bring herself to chastise the girl. "Your young man just delivered it personally," she said in a conspiratorial whisper.

"I don't have a young man Annie."

"Whatever you say Miss Gilbert, but where I come from if a fella takes you out for the evening and buys you a new dress, that means your courtin'."

"Well, if you put it that way – but do I need to ask how you know that this is a new dress?" Myra asked shaking the large oblong box at her.

"No Ma'am, he told me so. Said it would look lovely with your eyes, and would you consider wearing your hair down."

"Well, he is certainly impertinent," Myra chuckled. "And you should know better than to encourage such behavior."

"Oh Miss, he's ever so handsome and he seems to really like you a lot. Why not give yourself the chance?" Annie asked wisely as Myra opened the package. Inside was an elegant evening gown, in a deep blue with tiny seed pearly sewn all over the bodice and a swirling skirt that would swish and whisper with every step she took. "Oh my!"

"Oh my indeed Annie. Well, it would appear he has good taste."

"Try it on Miss, I can make any adjustments you need while you bathe."

Myra slipped out of her clothes and with Annie's help she stepped into the silk gown. It felt soft and cool against her skin, the cut accentuating her curves. She felt like a fairytale princess off to the ball to meet her Prince Charming. Annie began to dart around her, tucking and pinning swiftly. When she had finished the fit was perfect, and Myra almost broke down in tears. She barely looked like herself at all. "Miss Gilbert don't cry, you're beautiful," Annie said, her voice full of wonder.

"That is why I am crying, I never knew!"

"Tush, of course you did. Lovely lady like you. Only difference is a posh dress. Don't you be so silly. Now, get out of that carefully so as not to prick yourself and I'll run up the alterations sharpish."

Annie disappeared with the sumptuous gown as Myra sank into her warm bath. She played distractedly with the rose petals floating on the surface, and wondered if she was dreaming. Things like this simply did not happen to women like her. She was a dowdy spinster, and yet here she was being swept off her feet by a handsome stranger, showering her with gifts. It was delightful, but it wasn't real life and she needed to get to know the real Carlton Green – not just this chivalrous and romantic one. She couldn't make a decision to make her life with him based on his generosity alone.

When the time came, Myra could hardly believe it was her as she gazed upon her reflection. Annie had pinned her hair carefully so that curls escaped in a gentle froth from behind her ears, her blonde locks streaming down her back in a silken tangle. Annie had even shown her how to apply some simple makeup to enhance her eyelashes and make her eyes look enormous, and a little rouge on her cheeks and lips. The blue gown now fit her perfectly, and she looked just as beautiful as any of the women of quality she had ever seen. "Now, don't cry Miss, or you'll ruin it," Annie warned her as a tear had begun to threaten to appear. Annie wiped it carefully away.

"Thank you Annie. I don't know what to say."

"Don't say a thing Miss Gilbert, just go and have fun."

"Annie, call me Myra – I'm certainly no better than you in any way."

"Yes ma'am, you are. You're an educated lady, and I am a common maid. But, I will gladly call you Myra."

"Education is something I was lucky to receive because of who my Papa was – not because I am in any way your superior Annie. Don't ever let anyone tell you they are better than you because you are 'just' a maid.

You work hard, and have many skills – but even without them you have just as much right to be on this earth as anyone else." Annie grinned at her.

"Careful the bosses don't hear you teaching the girls things like that!" she warned.

"I should hope they already know that I have."

Chapter Five

The evening at the Opera had been magical. Myra had looked more perfect than Carlton could ever have imagined she would, and he had fallen head over heels in love with her as they discussed the quality of the production in the interval over a glass of wine. Myra was intelligent, sensitive and funny. He had enjoyed being with her more than he could ever have believed possible. Outings to the Zoological Gardens, museums and the theatre since had only convinced him that at last he had found the woman he would spend the rest of his life with.

He had begun to breathe just a little more easily with each outing they had undertaken where he had not bumped into anyone he had known before. It had been confusing, to be so excited and eager to see Myra, and yet to have his fears of discovery lurking in the back of his mind every time they were out. Today was the last day he could afford to spend here in Boston, and he had to admit he would be glad to not have to appear relaxed and carefree whilst constantly looking over his shoulder.

But, it also meant that today was the day that he and Myra would have to make a decision. He knew what he wanted that decision to be – but he was not sure if Myra felt the same way. Oh she was polite, and always seemed to be interested in his opinions. She laughed at his jokes and teased him more and more. But, it seemed that there was something in her that was holding her back too. He was sure her secret could be nothing like his own – but he was sure there was something. But, feeling optimistic he had planned this final outing down to the exact contents of the picnic basket he now carried on his arm.

"Would this be a spot you may consider?" Myra asked pointing to a spot under the shade of an old oak tree. He shook his head.

"I told you. I know exactly where I wish to take you," he said mysteriously.

"But we have almost run out of park!"

"Not at all. Though I am surprised that someone as curious as yourself has never found this place."

Myra gave him a wry smile and tucked her arm more tightly through his. He liked that she always wanted to walk arm in arm. He felt proud to be the one escorting her, and so the fact that she seemed to be proud to be with him made him happy.

He continued to tease her as they approached a wooden door tucked into the park wall. "See I told you we would run out of park," she scolded him.

"Nonsense," he said as he moved to open the door. She gasped as he stood back to let her enter in front of him. Before them was a beautiful garden, in the English style with formal box-hedging and blousy floral borders. It was a riot of color, and in the center was an elegant bandstand. He could hear the strains of a string quartet and smiled. He had wanted to ensure that everything was perfect, and the sweet romantic music just made it all the way he had planned for.

Myra's face was a picture of delight. He couldn't help but smile at how clever he had been to give her such a surprise. "However did you know of this place?" she asked.

"My Father proposed to my Mother here. I guess I wanted to uphold a little family tradition," he admitted as he put the picnic basket down on the steps of the bandstand, and knelt down upon one knee. "Dear Myra, will you marry me and return to Montana and make me the happiest man alive?"

"We shall need to marry here in Boston, or in Great Falls though, there is no church or chapel in Sun River yet, though I doubt it will be long before we build one," he said suddenly. She simply smiled at him and pulled him onto his feet, and standing on tip toe reached up to kiss him. He pulled her close to him, cradling her lithe body against his own and lost himself in her lips. He had so longed to claim them as his own, but had always held back. Now, here she was kissing him, setting him alight with passion, her eyes blazing with joy. Carlton had never felt so happy in his entire life.

* * * * *

Myra could hardly contain her happiness. She longed to shout it out to the entire world - that she was to marry this kind, generous and wonderfully handsome man. She had to stop herself from doing just that with every person they met in the Park as they made their way back home. Her eye kept being drawn back to the perfectly cut Sapphire on her ring finger, fiddling with it nervously as she got used to the weight of it on her hand. Carlton would just pat her hand gently where it lay on his arm, as if to reassure himself that she had said yes and was indeed wearing his ring.

"Be careful, you shall rub it away to nothing," Carlton teased her.

"I simply cannot believe that this has happened to me," she admitted.

"To us. I am so glad that you said yes, my love." The little endearment touched her more than she could ever have explained and she ducked her head into his chest to hide her blush. He kissed her on the crown, and smiled at her happily.

Couples and families smiled at them, as if sensing their news. Myra basked in the glow of their good feeling. Then as suddenly as everything had become perfect, it felt as if a cloud had covered the sun and doused them in the cold and harsh reality of life. Myra was not sure what had happened, nor if it was her fault – but Carlton suddenly went stiff, and unresponsive. "Carlton, are you quite well?"

"Of course," he replied tersely, his words and tone clipped and distant. All of a sudden she was confronted with a man she simply did not know. She longed to ask what had happened to make him so aloof – but she did not dare. His face, usually so open and full of laughter, was like a closed book. She looked around them, trying to see if there was a clue, anything at all that could tell her why the man she loved had become a complete stranger to her – and as she followed his gaze she saw an elderly gentleman, playing with a young boy. He could not have been more than ten years old, and they were playing with a wonderful sail boat on the lake. "Carlton, do you know them?" she asked tentatively. Carlton just kept staring.

"Carlton, please talk to me! Whatever is the matter? Who are they to you? Why do you look so stern?"

"Myra stop fussing. It is not important. I shall escort you home immediately. Please, do not ever speak of this again." Myra nodded, unwillingly. Clearly something about the pair had unsettled Carlton, but she could not force him to confide in her. She would be patient, would let him come to her when he was ready. She prayed that he would be one day. She did not want there to be secrets between them, especially not now. But she had the worst feeling that this was something that could drive a wedge between them that may never heal.

"I shall come by at ten o'clock in the morning," he said briskly. "My train leaves at eleven. Should you wish to accompany me immediately, or would you like to wait and serve out your notice?"

"I should like to come with you, but I must wait and at least say my goodbyes to the girls. It will give you time to have the banns read so we can wed as soon as I arrive," she said gently. He nodded, bent his head and gave her a chaste peck on the cheek.

"Until the morning then."

"But, what of supper tonight? Cook has prepared your favorite-roast beef?" she asked, feeling tears of confusion and unhappiness pricking at the back of her eyes.

35

"Please make my apologies. I have something I must attend to after all."

With that he marched down the steps and then swiftly down the street and out of sight. Myra stared after him. How could the most wonderful thing to ever happen to her have soured so fast? Overwhelmed and unsure if he even wanted to marry her now, she sank to the floor and sobbed.

Chapter Six

Carlton stormed past the elderly butler and into the impressive hallway. He was not going to leave without some answers. He knew he had made terrible mistakes, but he did not deserve this, to find out such a thing in such a way. "Havershall, you damned dog. Where are you? Come out and face me you coward?" he yelled up the stairs.

"Sir, Mr Havershall is not at home."

"He damn well is, I just saw him come in." Carlton growled. "Now, you can tell me where he is Galen, or I will break down every door in the place." The butler shuddered, but pointed to the library.

"Thank you. I'm sorry to scare you, none of this is your fault my old friend."

"Young Master Carlton, your Father is an old man – like I am. What he did, he did for a reason I'm sure."

"Why didn't you tell me? Why didn't Mother tell me?"

"How could we young Sir?" Carlton had to agree with that. How could an employee, a wife go against the head of the household. But this was too important to have kept silence – whatever it may have cost them. "I was in no position to do so, and well your Mother died four years ago. I thought he would have at least written to you and told you. I shouldn't say – but I think she died of a broken heart. She was never the same after you and Miss Abigail well…," he tailed off unsure what to say next.

"Mother is dead?" Carlton stared at the old butler dumbfounded. For a moment he had been about to give his Father the excuse that he hadn't known where he was to let him know – but he was sure that his dear Papa would have known exactly where he had been from the moment he left the house, tormented by grief all those years ago. The man never let anything get past him.

He burst into the library, and stared at the image he was greeted with. His Father was sat on the settle, the young boy curled up by his side reading a book. It brought back so many memories of having done the same thing with his Father as a child. There had been many such happy days, before he had been sent away to boarding school to be prepared to enter the family dynasty.

"Run along Benjy, I need to talk to this gentleman in private," his Father said warmly. The boy looked up at his Grandfather with eyes as green as Carlton's own. He obeyed unquestioningly, but his intrigue level had clearly been piqued as he gave the intruder into his world a thorough looking over as he walked past.

"You told me he was dead Father," he said nodding at the door the boy had left through.

"And you told me you would never return to Boston."

"There is a massive difference in expecting me to stay away from the scene of such heartbreak – and you never telling me I didn't need to be half as unhappy! He's my son Father, and you told me he was dead. You allowed me to think I had killed him – and Abigail."

"I did what I thought was best."

"By depriving us both of nine years together? In what twisted world does that make sense?"

"You drove your wife to her death. I would not take the risk that you would do the same to my grandson. I shall never let you do the same to him. He believes that you are dead. I intend him to never know anything different."

"So you still believe that Abigail took her own life because I mistreated her?"

"What other reason could she have had?"

"I don't know Father, but I am fed up of trying to work out why. I am also fed up of blaming myself. I treated Abigail well. She never loved me, never wanted to marry me – she did so to please her Father who didn't care one whit about her happiness, only that he create an alliance with you. Well I hope all the money you made together was worth knowing that a kind and gentle woman took her life to escape the life the pair of you created for her. I will not let you do the same to my son. You will not manipulate his life like you did mine, or his Mother's."

"You can do nothing," his Father sneered. "Look at you, you can't hope to win against my wealth, my contacts – not here in Boston."

"Well then, it is as well that I don't live in Boston isn't it. If it takes me the rest of my life, my boy will be coming home with me. I won't have him thinking that this," Carlton looked around the cavernous room disparagingly, "is everything there is to life."

"If you wish to lose, then so be it. You shall never take him from me."

Carlton turned and stormed out of the room. He should have known better than to try and bait the dragon in his own lair, but seeing them like that in the Park had been too much of a shock. His Father had told him that Abigail had taken not only her own life, but Benjamin's too. He had been utterly devastated, and had blamed himself for their loss. But he had thought about it all so hard and so long, for so many years up in his desolate isolation. He had probably been the only person to ever show Abigail even one iota of kindness. He hadn't loved her, not the way he did Myra, but that didn't mean he hadn't been tender towards her. Benjamin had been such a blessing – to them both. He had so prayed that their son would be enough to help her to find enough joy to stay with them. She had always been so melancholy, a pawn in the game of two powerful men who thought that people could be used for their own ends.

Well, he would avenge her death for them by ensuring that Benjamin had a better life – one full of love and joy. He would fight his Father with every penny he had, would even sell the farm if needs be – but he would not abandon his boy to the soul-less world in which his Father lived. But, he had just proposed marriage to Myra, and she knew nothing of his past. He couldn't expect her to marry him and then be saddled with a ten year old boy she hadn't known existed. He couldn't expect her to even want him after the way he had treated her this afternoon.

* * * * *

Whoever was knocking on the door was clearly determined to gain access, Myra thought as she listened anxiously to the heavy pounding. Nobody ever called at this hour, and the entire house had been readying themselves for bed. She clutched her dressing gown around her and made her way downstairs. She peeked out of the window on the landing and saw Carlton there. He looked distraught. She rushed down the final flight of stairs and beckoning to Cook and Annie to go back to bed she opened the door.

"Carlton, whatever is the matter? You have the entire house scared out of their wits?"

"Myra, I am so very sorry, but I must break off our engagement," he said hurriedly, tears flooding down his face.

"Now, don't be so silly. Come in. Nothing so bad can have happened in just a few hours that means we need to rethink our plans," she said pragmatically, though her insides were churning with fear. She simply couldn't bear the thought of losing him, not now she knew without doubt that she loved him with all her heart.

"I'm sorry, I can't tell you."

"Yes you can, and you will. That is what wives are for – to help you shoulder the burdens," she reminded him adamantly.

"You will never forgive me, you are better off without me, everyone is." Myra was stunned by the maudlin tone, and the defeatist language.

"This has something to do with the old man and the boy we saw in the park doesn't it? Now, I'm guessing he must be your son. Now, my brain can go on a little jaunt to try and workout what is going on here – or you can give me the quick version. I'd hate to end up with something completely wrong and I probably would as I have a very fertile imagination," she said with a gentle smile as she tenderly wiped away his tears, and kissed him on the mouth.

"You don't mind that I have a son?" he asked incredulously.

"Not in the least, why ever should I?"

"Because I didn't tell you about him, or that I was married before," he said as if it were the most obvious thing in the world.

"Carlton, I am not so naive as to think that at your age you have never had a relationship with a woman before me. What matters to me is our future, not your past."

"Yes, I was married. It was arranged by my father. Poor Abigail was so unhappy. She and I, well we weren't well suited and though I cared for her as best I could and she tried she just got more and more unhappy. I blamed myself. When Benjamin was born we both hoped things would get better, but she just got more unhappy than ever. She took her own life."

"Oh Carlton, that must have been so terrible for you to bear. I'll wager you blamed yourself and went off to lick your wounds in the wilds of some far off place, like Montana?" she said, very gently teasing him.

"I haven't told you the worst part. My Father told me Abigail had killed Benjamin too." Myra had nothing to say to such cruelty. She stared at him, then took his hands between her own.

"Then we need to make sure that your son is taken away from such a monster, and finds out that he has a Father who loves him and a stepmother who will too."

"I cannot ask that of you. It is too much."

"No it isn't. Now, my Father may be dead but he had some very influential friends. He taught most of Boston's legal profession. I am sure we can find someone who will be more than happy to help us to get your boy back."

"Myra Gilbert, I do not know what I ever did to deserve you, but I am so glad that I found you. You truly are a marvel, a treasure, the most wonderful creature I have ever known!"

"You are just a little punch-drunk right now my love, but thank you for the lovely compliments. Now, get back to the hotel and get a good night's rest. Then go to the station and amend your ticket so we can hire a lawyer before you go back to Montana, and I shall try and find somewhere where we can marry right away. I am not ever going to leave your side again."

Chapter Seven

Myra still did not know if Carlton loved her, but she knew she would do anything for him. His revelations of the night before had done nothing to change that. She prayed he would one day come to love her with all his heart, but she was more than happy to accept his pleasant companionship and obvious physical attraction towards her. She prayed that they would find a way to reunite father and son once more, maybe if she could do that for them it would be enough to make him love her too.

She hurried out of the house at first light, to visit with Reverend Cartwright. She was sure there must be some way that she and Carlton could be married today. The kindly man was more than happy to help her out, and agreed to read the banns in the morning service and marry them after evensong. It wasn't the dream wedding that every girl planned and hoped for, but she would be walking down the aisle with the man who held her heart and that was more than most could ever hope for.

She then rushed to Uncle Peter's chambers. He had been Papa's closest friend, and was now a Judge. If he didn't know what they could do next, then no man alive could help them. She had told Carlton to meet her there, and as she rounded the corner and saw him waiting for her, kicking nervously at the step her heart filled with love. She rushed towards him, and was overjoyed when he took her in his arms and bent his head down to kiss her passionately on the lips. "You are sure you want to help me with this?"

"Of course, and we shall be married after evensong, so I shall have to!" she quipped.

"I am so glad you did not turn away from me. I blamed myself for so long for Abigail's death, my son's death – but I shall never do so again. Shall place the blame where it truly lies – with my Father and hers."

"Good." She ushered him inside and they were shown into Uncle Peter's office. He stood up and hugged her warmly.

"How can I help you my dear?" he asked. She indicated that Carlton should tell his entire sorry tale.

Myra watched as Uncle Peter made notes, occasionally querying the points Carlton made. He listened so attentively, and she could see her fiancé begin to relax and feel at ease with him. When Carlton finished speaking he carefully reviewed the notes, then looked up at them. "Well, this should be relatively straightforward," he said. Myra and Carlton looked at one another, and heaved a sigh of relief. "Your Father has no rights to the boy if you are still alive and no charges have ever been pressed against you. The fact that Myra intends to marry you will stand you in good stead amongst a good three quarters of the legal profession in this city, and the other quarter are in the pockets of those men like your Father. If we can get this before the right judge, and quickly, I see no reason why you shouldn't be able to take your boy home with you immediately. The quicker we act, the less time your Father has to try and subvert us."

"Truly?" Carlton asked. "I can hardly believe it. I only found out he was alive yesterday, and he could be coming home with us tomorrow?"

"If I can manage it, maybe even today!" Peter said as he shook Carlton's hand. He hugged Myra close. "I'll be in touch."

They walked out of his chambers hand in hand, and made their way back to Young's Hotel where Carlton had been staying. They went into the restaurant and ordered a celebratory lunch, but both of them were too nervous to eat much of it. They knew there were still too many hurdles to climb before they truly had their happily ever after.

* * * * *

A note was delivered to them as they sat drinking their coffee. "Uncle Peter says we should be at the courthouse at half past two," Myra said reading the note carefully. The look of hope on her face was adorable, and Carlton leant over to kiss her gently. He checked his pocket watch, and seeing it was almost a quarter to two they got up and he helped her into her coat. The court house was not far, but the streets could be busy and this was too important to miss.

When they arrived there Peter was waiting with a young man by his side. Myra clearly recognized him, and Carlton was rocked by jealousy as he watched her embrace him affectionately. "Carlton, this is my Father's favorite pupil, Myles Clannon. Papa used to say he was a genius."

"I was never as clever as you Myra, if I'd ever had to stand and face you in a court I shouldn't stand a chance!" His flirtatious and over familiar tone grated on Carlton, and he longed to punch this new intruder rather than to take his advice – but he knew he had to accept the man's help. His boy needed a father who loved him – not a Grandfather who would use him eventually for his own gain.

"Are you ready? Peter told me all about your case. This really should be very simple and we should be able to serve your Father with the court's decision almost immediately." Carlton choked down his envy, and managed to smile at the man. He really was grateful for how kind everyone was being. But he couldn't help longing for his home, the peace and quiet. It would be wonderful when he, Myra and Benjamin could return there.

"I think so," he said cautiously, trying not to get his hopes up too high.

His father hadn't even bothered to come. His lawyers sat at their table looking puffed up and important, and so very arrogant that Carlton prayed Myra's faith in Myles Clannon was justified. The Judge was called, and when he saw Peter's smiling face enter the courtroom suddenly all his fears evaporated. Just thirty minutes later he and Myra walked out of the courtroom, arm in arm, clutching the court's decision.

"Just because you have a piece of paper does not mean you take the boy from his home, from the people he loves!" his Father said looking flustered.

"That is exactly what it means Father. I know you thought that your money could buy you everything you want – but not this time I'm afraid. Now, where is the boy? Where is Benjamin?"

"I shall appeal!"

"And you shall have to do so in Montana, which is where we shall be. If you ever wish to see Benjamin again, I suggest you learn to live with this court's decision Father. I shall be happy for you to come and visit if you choose – but I shall never trust you with my boy. You will not make his life as unhappy as you made mine and Abigail's."

The old man crumpled in front of Carlton's eyes, but he could feel no pity for him. He looked up as he heard footsteps on the stairs. Benjamin was standing on the third step. "Is it true? You are my Father?"

"Yes Benjamin," Carlton said frankly. Myra squeezed his hand. He was so glad she was by his side.

"Why did they tell me you were dead?"

"My Father did what he thought was best, for you and for me. But he forgot one vital part of that – that it is best to ask people what they want and need before deciding for them." His Father winced, and in that moment Carlton was sure that he would never need anything more than that.

"Did you not want me?"

"I have always wanted you. I have grieved for nine long years thinking you were dead too. Had I known, I would never have left you."

"I must come and live with you now?" his little face was so earnest. Carlton nodded.

"If you want to. If you would rather stay here in Boston with your Grandfather then I would understand. I am a stranger after all."

"No, I want to come with you. I don't like living here. I love

Grandfather, but I don't want to go to boarding school. You won't send me away will you?"

"No my dear boy, never."

Epilogue

The church was full. As Myra peeked through the doors she was amazed that so many people were here at such short notice. She almost cried as she saw Carlton standing at the altar with his handsome son by his side. The two were smiling at one another, Carlton's arm loosely about the lad's shoulders. It was almost as if they had never been parted. Annie quickly dabbed at her eyes and carefully placed her veil over her face. "You look lovely Myra," she said, her voice a little choked.

"Thank you."

The organ started up and she took Uncle Peter's arm and walked slowly down the aisle towards the man she loved. She proudly promised to love him and honor him, and couldn't keep the smile from her face as they walked back down the aisle as man and wife. "Well, I have to say life with you is never dull," she teased. Carlton kissed her tenderly.

"I truly hope it will be a little quieter once we get home!"

"Indeed, now will I be living in a sod cabin, or that lovely house you told me all about?"

"I have no idea – I suppose we will find out when we get there!

But, wherever we end up, I want you to know just how much I love you Mrs Green. You have changed my life, helped me get back my son, and you are more precious than anything else on earth."

"Except Benjamin, of course," she reminded him, but she could feel the blush on her cheeks and her heart fill with love at the truth in his words. "I love you too, and I am afraid you are stuck with us both forever now.

"I can't think of anything more wonderful," he admitted and kissed her again.

The train journey had been fun. Benjy had very much enjoyed learning all about how the engines worked from the drivers and firemen. Every evening at dinner he regaled them of his adventures, and insisted that when he was older he was going to work on the railways too. She had laughed as Carlton had smiled and told him that whatever he wanted to do was fine by her, though it was clear he wasn't sure how safe it would be. But, he had been more than happy to trust the kindly men with his son as Benjy had been determined to spend much of his days assisting them. Myra didn't complain, it had meant that she and Carlton had been able to spend some time alone, and they had enjoyed getting to know one another as man and wife. She certainly had no doubts now as to whether or not he loved her.

She had enjoyed the long train journey, she had never known how very different all the States were. They passed through green fields, red dust, desert, plains and mountains on their cross country adventure. But when they reached the borders of Montana she gasped out loud at just how beautiful it was. She could never have imagined anything quite so perfect, and it made her feel small to witness such majestic mountains. Their snow-capped peaks made it seem almost unreal, as if she had stepped into a picture book – but this was to be her home now.

She and Benjy had stood patiently waiting as Carlton arranged to borrow a neighbor's buggy so they could drive home in comfort. He had already warned them that they still had quite a way to go from the station in Great Falls. But, both were excited and eager to see more of their new home. Once their trunks were strapped firmly onto the backboard, they set off at a gentle trot. Myra marveled at the rock strewn river that guided them along their way. The track was a little rutted, and took them up into the foothills, then back down onto the valley floor.

"My farm is just up around the next bend," Carlton said excitedly. "I wonder what we shall be sleeping in tonight?"

"Well, I'd say Ardloe has been busy!" Myra said, relief in her voice as they rounded the bend. A smart clapboard dwelling now stood where his old sod cabin had once been.

"Is that our house?" Benjamin said, his eyes wide with wonder.

"I think it just might be?" Carlton said ruffling the lad's curls. "Do you like it Mrs Green?"

"It'll do," she said with a grin. "I just hope he remembered the indoor outhouse!"

"Oh, I told him you insisted on electricity too – we are going to be the fanciest farmers in the valley!"

"Why don't you go and explore Benjy," she said as the gig came to a stop. He raced off and only his foot thuds could be heard as he rushed onto the broad porch.

"So, what do you think of Montana, wife?"

"I think you were right about those beautiful mountains, and that the peace is so welcoming and wonderful. And you were right about this beautiful house. I truly do love it. Thank you husband, this is going to be such a wonderful place to bring up a family."

"It is perfect now," he admitted as he pulled her against him and kissed her. "It was always just a little bit lonely before, but I doubt that I will ever feel that way ever again."

The End

Thank you for reading and supporting my book and I hope you enjoyed it.

Please will you do me a favor and leave a review so I'll know whether you liked it or not, it would be very much appreciated, thank you.

Other books by Karla

SUN RIVER BRIDES SERIES

A bride for Carlton #1
A bride for Mackenzie #2
A bride for Ethan #3
A bride for Thomas #4
A bride for Mathew #5

About Karla Gracey

Karla Gracey was born with a very creative imagination and a love for creating stories that will inspire and warm people's hearts. She has always been attracted to historical romance including mail order bride stories with strong willed women. Her characters are easy to relate to and you feel as if you know them personally. Whether you enjoy action, adventure, romance, mystery, suspense or drama- she makes sure there is something for everyone in her historical romance stories!

Made in the USA
Las Vegas, NV
06 June 2021

24290217R00038